THIS WALKER BOOK BELONGS TO:

_____

_____

_____

_____

**For Donna, Janine,
Michael, Nina,
Amy, and Malcolm**

First published 1986
by Julia MacRae Books
This edition published 1989
by Walker Books Ltd
87 Vauxhall Walk
London SE11 5HJ

Printed in Italy by Lito di Roberto Terrazzi

British Library Cataloguing in Publication Data
Jonas, Ann
Now we can go.
I. Title
813'.54[J] PZ7
ISBN 0-7445-1330-8

NOW WE CAN GO

A MEMORY GAME
FOR YOUNG CHILDREN

ANN JONAS

WALKER BOOKS
LONDON

Wait a minute!
I'm not ready.

I need my bag,

my ball,

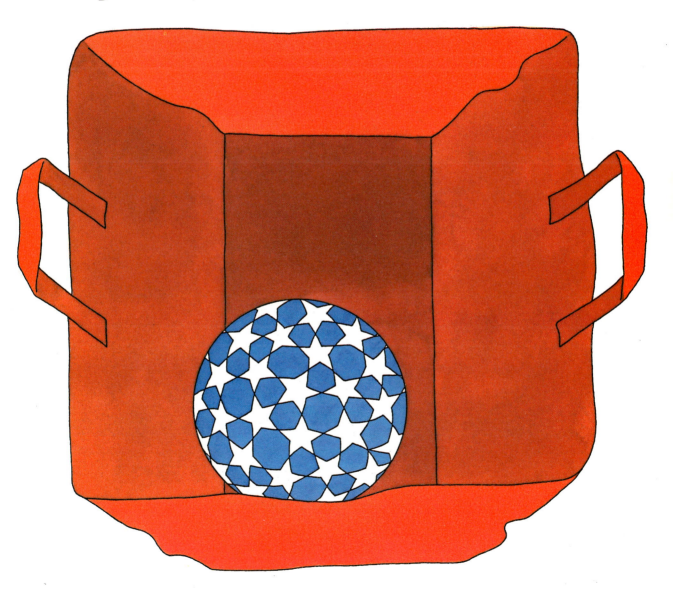

my skates,

my boat,

my doll,

my book,

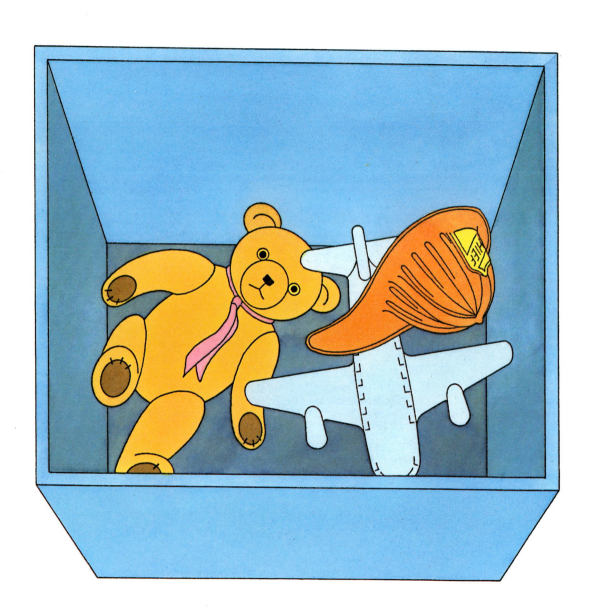

my truck,

my hat,

my aeroplane,

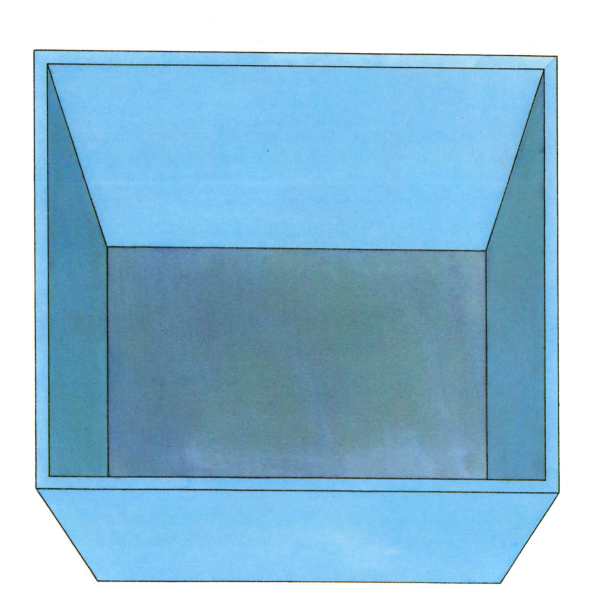

and my bear.

Now we can go!

MORE WALKER PAPERBACKS

BABIES' FIRST BOOKS
Jan Ormerod
Little ones
JUST LIKE ME
SILLY GOOSE   OUR OLLIE

PICTURE BOOKS
For the very young

Helen Oxenbury
Pippo
No.1 TOM & PIPPO READ A STORY
No.2 TOM & PIPPO MAKE A MESS
No.3 TOM & PIPPO GO FOR A WALK
No.4 TOM & PIPPO AND THE
    WASHING MACHINE
No.5 TOM & PIPPO GO SHOPPING
No.6 TOM & PIPPO'S DAY
No.7 TOM & PIPPO IN THE GARDEN
No.8 TOM & PIPPO SEE THE MOON

Nicola Bayley
NONSENSE RHYMES

LEARNING FOR FUN
The Pre-School Years

Shirley Hughes
Nursery Collection
NOISY
COLOURS
BATHWATER'S HOT
ALL SHAPES AND SIZES
TWO SHOES, NEW SHOES
WHEN WE WENT TO THE PARK

John Burningham
Concept Books
COLOURS   ALPHABET
OPPOSITES   NUMBERS

Philippe Dupasquier
Busy Places
THE GARAGE   THE AIRPORT
THE BUILDING SITE
THE FACTORY   THE HARBOUR
THE RAILWAY STATION